Received On
OCT 2 3 2015
Ballard Branch
D0466510

For Jason and Steven —E.P.

For my brothers, cave building experts —S.G.

Farrar Straus Giroux Books for Young Readers
175 Fifth Avenue, New York 10010

Text copyright © 2015 by Eric Pinder
Pictures copyright © 2015 by Stephanie Graegin
All rights reserved

Color separations by Embassy Graphics
Printed in China by RR Donnelley Asia Printing Solutions Ltd.,
Dongguan City, Guangdong Province
Designed by Roberta Pressel
First edition, 2015
1 3 5 7 9 10 8 6 4 2

mackids.com

Library of Congress Cataloging-in-Publication Data
Pinder, Eric, 1970–
How to share with a bear / Eric Pinder ; pictures by Stephanie Graegin.
—First edition.
pages cm
Summary: One cold day, Thomas builds a cave of pillows and blankets where he can read, but when he goes to get a flashlight, a young "bear" goes inside and nothing Thomas does discourages the bear from being near him.
ISBN 978-0-374-30019-7 (hardcover)
[1. Bears—Fiction. 2. Brothers—Fiction.] I. Graegin, Stephanie, illustrator. II. Title.

PZ7.P63235How 2015
[E]—dc23

2014032835

Farrar Straus Giroux Books for Young Readers may be purchased for business or promotional use.
For information on bulk purchases please contact Macmillan Corporate and Premium Sales Department at (800) 221-7945 x5442 or by email at specialmarkets@macmillan.com.

HOW TO SHARE WITH A BEAR

ERIC PINDER
Pictures by STEPHANIE GRAEGIN

Farrar Straus Giroux New York

One cold day, Thomas gathered some pillows and blankets and made a warm, cozy cave.

The cave was too dark to read in, so Thomas went to get a flashlight. When he returned, he could hear something bump and thump and move around in the cave.

Something big.

Thomas peered inside.
Two shy brown eyes stared back.

It was a bear!

Everyone knows that bears like berries, so Thomas made a trail of blueberries leading away from the cave.

Then he waited.

Sniff. Snort. Snuff.

Soon enough, the bear bumbled through the hall, bustled down the stairs, and disappeared.

Quick as he could, Thomas got his favorite books and rushed back to the cave.

Too late!

The bear was already there. Caves never stay empty for long.

Bears love to scratch their backs on trees, so Thomas found his mom's wooden back scratcher, gave himself a good scratching, then set the scratcher down outside his bedroom door.

The bear shuffled
out to grab it.

Scritch.
Scrooch.
Scratch.

Thomas crawled into his cave and started to read, until a floating tuft of bear fur tickled his nose.

Achoo!

He went to get a tissue.

When he turned around, the bear was in the cave again.

Bears love to fish in streams,
so Thomas filled the sink and
dropped in some bath toys.

The bear came running.

Thomas barely got comfortable in his cave before he heard a new noise.

Gurgle. Burble. Plink.

The bear must have turned the water back on. Thomas went to shut the faucet off.

The bear passed him in the hall.

Bears like honey, so Thomas set out a bowl of honey oat cereal in the kitchen. He put on his honeybee costume and said *BZZZZ!* as loud as he could.

Then he dashed away flapping his arms, leading the bear downstairs.

The bear smelled the honey and stopped to gobble up the cereal, while Thomas hurried to his cave. At last he could read!

That's when the bear came back.

When he saw Thomas in the cave, he tried to snuggle in next to him. But the cave was too small. The bear started to cry.

Thomas felt sad for tricking the bear. "You can read, too," he told him. "Come and look." Thomas tried to make more room by pushing out the walls.

CAVE-IN!

Thomas poked his head out. The bear giggled. Thomas grinned. "Let's build a bigger cave," he said. "We can share."

Thomas huddled with the bear in their big new cave.

They shared a bowl of blueberries.

They shared a good book.

And Thomas learned that bears like one thing even more than fish or blueberries or honey.

They like their big brothers.

How to Build a Cave

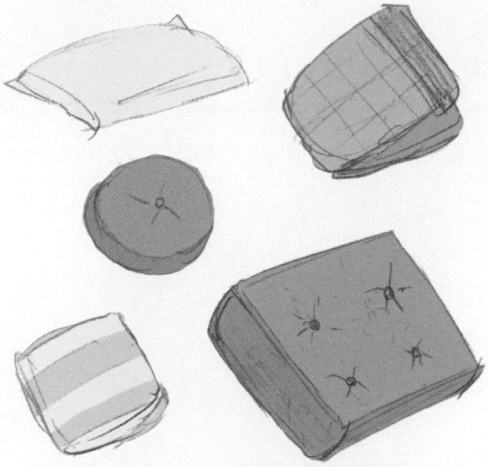

1. Gather all the pillows, cushions, and blankets you can, and bring them to the site of your cave.

2. Use the largest pillows and cushions to construct your walls. Lean them against one another. Use smaller pillows as inside support.

3. Use the blankets and lighter pillows to make your roof.

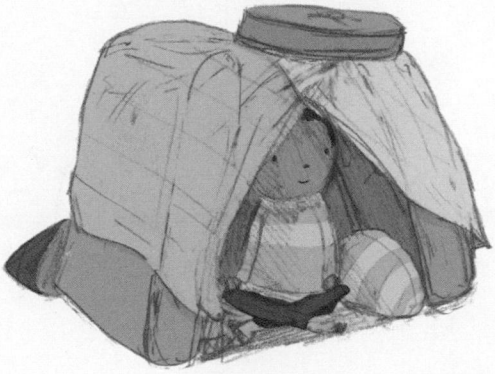

4. Enjoy your cave!